Firefly Fourth of July

by Elaine Reynolds and Cindy Jarrett
Illustrated by Logan Rogers

Gypsy
Publications

Published in 2018, by Gypsy Publications
Troy, OH 45373, U.S.A.
www.GypsyPublications.com

Reynolds, Elaine & Jarrett, Cindy
Firefly Fourth of July
story by Elaine Reynolds & Cindy Jarrett
Illustrated by Logan Rogers

First Edition

ISBN 978-1-938768-83-5 (hardback)
ISBN 978-1-938768-82-8 (paperback)

Library of Congress Control Number
2018952738

Book Design by Tim Rowe

This book is dedicated to our families who
are the lights of our lives.

Elaine's husband: Norm

Elaine's sons and daughters-in-law:
Ryan & Kim and Devin & Michele

Elaine's grandchildren:
Joe, Nathan, Sam, Andrew, and Mason

Cindy's husband: Bob

Cindy's sons and daughters-in-law:
Jeff & Tammy, Jason, and Jeremy & Jessica

Cindy's grandchildren:
Jordan, Jonathan, Jacob, Jasmine, Jewel, Joey,
Teagan, and Javin

Every year on the Fourth of July firefly families come out to play. Fireworks, picnics, and get-togethers with friends--all these things made Sunny twinkle with excitement! She couldn't wait!

Staying cool was the aim of the day! The sun sizzled, and the plants drooped. Sunny decided to spend it in the shade of a Daisy with her best friend, Flash. But the plants were not the only thing drooping. Flash looked absolutely frazzled!

"What's wrong with you?" asked Sunny in dismay.
"My light won't shine! Everyone will be flashing theirs, and I can't get mine to glow!" exclaimed Flash. "What am I going to do?"

"Relax, and it will light!" replied Sunny.

"I already tried," Flash wailed. "It just won't shine! What else can I do?"

Sunny thought for a minute, then started to tickle Flash.
"What are you doing?" giggled Flash.
"I'm trying to make you light up with laughter!" said Sunny.
"Stop! My problem isn't funny, and this isn't working!"
yelled Flash. "Try something else!"

"Try flying upside down," Sunny replied.

"Ok," answered Flash. So he turned upside down and whirled in circles. Faster and faster he went until he began to feel very peculiar. He was spinning so violently he tumbled out of the air and landed on his head!

"Ouch!" yelled Flash. "All that did was make me dizzy!"

Other fireflies arrived to see what the commotion was all about. One firefly whispered quietly to the others, "Let's scare his light on."

So, when Flash wasn't looking, they all screamed, "Boo!"
"You frightened the daylights out of me!" yelled Flash.
"We're sorry," they said. "We were just trying to help."

"Have you tried soaking up the sun's rays? Humans do that, and they turn every color from tan to bright red. Maybe that will work."

"All right," said Flash. "Promise you won't scare me again, and I'll try." So he flew to the beach and lay out in the sun. Before long, Flash felt uncomfortably warm. His face turned frightfully red, and his wings sizzled and smoldered!

"Ok," answered Flash. "What now?"

"We are called lightning bugs. Maybe flying close to a lightning strike will work."

"That sounds dangerous!" whimpered Flash. "I'll only go if you come, too."

So they joined hands and bravely approached a thunder storm.

Before long, a flash of lightning electrified the air! A spark of light traveled through Flash's hand to each of his friends. When it was over, they agreed it had been a shocking experience, but still no light could be seen in Flash's tail.

Tired of everyone's brilliant ideas, Flash decided it was time to see a doctor. So Sunny and Flash flew off to see specialist Dr. Luci Ferin.

After examining Flash, Dr. Ferin said, "There's nothing wrong with your light. You have a bad case of the 'worry bug blues.'"

"What's that?" asked Flash.

"Are you hearing the words 'I can't do this? I can't do that' in your head?"

"Yes," admitted Flash. "Is there a cure?"

"Yes. Follow this prescription to chase the 'worry bug' away."

Dr. Ferin handed Flash a paper that read:

**Office of
Dr. Luci Ferin**

Step 1. Believe in yourself.
If you believe in yourself, you can
do anything.

Step 2. Every time you hear the 'worry bug'
speak in your head, say these words
loudly: "Go away 'worry bug'. Leave
me alone. My light is fine. I know
it will shine."

Step 3. Repeat until you believe it.

Step 4. Relax, and enjoy
the Fourth of July.

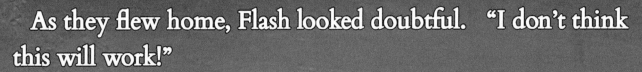

As they flew home, Flash looked doubtful. "I don't think this will work!"

"That's the 'worry bug' talking," warned Sunny. "But never fear, our firefly friends will help you," and they did just that! Each time Flash worried, they all chanted, "My light is fine. I know it will shine."

On the Fourth, they flew to Fireworks Park. As the brilliant lights began to explode overhead, Flash and his firefly friends took to the sky with hopeful determination.

The next morning Flash's picture was on the front page, and the headline read: "Extraordinary Light Display Illuminates the Night Sky," but it wasn't talking about the fireworks.

FIREFLY GAZETTE
Extraordinary Light Display Illuminates the Night Sky!

Best Fourth of July Ever!

Who knew fireflies could create such a spectacular display? Flash and friends were the heroes of the night, delivering the best light show ever, and Flash's light was the brightest of all!

FASCINATING FIREFLY FACTS

1. Fireflies are beetles, not flies.

2. The four stages of a firefly's life are egg (3-4 weeks), larva (1-3 years), pupa (10 days), and adult (5-30 days). Fireflies hibernate during the larval stage, some species for several years.

3. The larvae of fireflies eat snails, worms, and slugs that destroy crops and infect humans with disease.

4. Understanding how a firefly glows resulted in the creation of glow sticks and toys that light up.

5. Firefly blood contains chemicals, Luciferin and Luciferase, which taste bitter, so many animals avoid eating them.

6. Fireflies aren't poisonous to humans, and they don't bite, attack, or carry disease.

7. While fireflies in some areas flash yellow, some members of the species flash green, orange, red, or blue.

8. Fireflies in the western United States can't flash at all. Fireflies inhabit every continent except Antarctica.

9. Firefly populations are dwindling all over the world due to light pollution, the use of insecticides, and construction on firefly breeding sites.

REFERENCES

Firefly Life Cycle: https://www.thoughtco.com/life-cycle-fireflies-lightning-bugs-1968137

Ten Fascinating Facts About Fireflies: https://www.thoughtco.com/fascinating-facts-about-fireflies-1968117

How Do Fireflies Light?: https://www.thoughtco.com/how-do-fireflies-light-1968122

Fireflies: 12 Things You Didn't Know About Fireflies: https://www.mnn.com/earth-matters/animals/stories/fireflies-12-things-you-didnt-know-about-lightning-bugs

Beneficials in the Garden, Firefly/Lightning Bug: http://aggie-horticulture.tamu.edu/galveston/beneficials/beneficial-40_lightning_bug.html

"Fireflies": http://ncase.me/fireflies/

What Do Fireflies Eat?: https://newengland.com/today/living/gardening/what-do-fireflies-eat/

Why Do Fireflies Glow?: https://www.almanac.com/content/fireflies-why-do-fireflies-glow

Facts About Fireflies: http://www.firefly.org/facts-about-fireflies.html

Bug Index – Firefly: http://www.beneficialbugs.org/bugs/Firefly/boreal_firefly.html

Glowing, Glowing, Gone: – Why Fireflies Are Disappearing and What You Can Do to Help: http://www.firefly.org/

CPSIA information can be obtained
at www.ICGtesting.com
Printed in the USA
LVHW07s0404010918
588842LV00003B/3/P